Dear Black Child

By Rahma Rodaah Illustrated by Lydia Mba

BALZER + BRAY
An Imprint of HarperCollins Publishers

Balzer + Bray is an imprint of HarperCollins Publishers.

Dear Black Child
Text copyright © 2022 by Rahma Rodaah
Illustrations copyright © 2022 by Lydia Mba
All rights reserved. Manufactured in Italy.
ISBN 978-0-06-309197-9

The artist used Adobe Photoshop and Procreate to create the digital illustrations for this book.
Typography by Dana Fritts
Hand lettering by Kristle Marshall
22 23 24 25 26   RTLO   10 9 8 7 6 5 4 3 2 1
❖
First Edition

To Hoyo and Abbo,
who sacrificed everything to make our dreams possible.
And to all Black children who feel unseen, know that you matter!
I see you and I love you!

−R.R.

To my nephews, Aday and Daniele.

−L.M.

Dear Black child,

The universe is vast.

So take up as much space as you can.

Stand in your own light.
Wear your crown with pride.

Let your name be your flag.
Say it loud and say it proud.
Wave it until it's woven in their mind.

Proclaim your native tongue as the national anthem.
Form your own band.

Roam freely—you need no permission to be on this land.

Taking up space demands you speak confidently.
So fill your lungs with air and let your voice echo
from every corner.

Be rooted, but move as swiftly as a river.

Taking up space means feeling at ease wherever you are.

Do not fear the unknown.
Instead, pave the way for others to follow.

When you enter, do not fold yourself in half,
hoping to go unnoticed. Dare to stand tall.

If you don't see yourself included in the history books,
pick up your pen and tell the world your story.

The one that only you can tell.

Life is rarely without storms. The wind may roar with hurtful words from those who fear you. And sometimes when it rains, it pours.

Rise and meet the tides! Drape yourself in courage and create sunlight where there is none.
When in doubt, use your inner compass to lead you home.

There are places that will always welcome you.
There are people who will open their borders
and hearts to you—who will make you feel
safe and loved.

They are your lighthouse.
Your refuge when you feel lost at sea.

Gather your strength and march on.

Dear Black child,

We are here to remind you of your glory.

You are **Worthy**.

You are **Enough**.

You **Belong**.

This **Space** was created for you.

Because you are a walking nation,
a monument, and a true gift to this world.

And we can't wait to witness how your presence will shape our future.

This is just the beginning.